Pete's Peculiar Pet Sl

CW00841476

The Very Smelly Dragon

Contents

Written by Sheila May Bird

Illustrated by Jim Field

Chapter 1
Burp!

Pete, the owner of Pete's Peculiar Pet Shop, was returning to his shop. As he was passing the entrance to a cave, something shot out of it and landed at his feet. It was a baby dragon.

The dragon looked up at Pete with big, sad eyes.

Pete gently picked up the dragon and
carried it back to his shop.

Pete put a large sign in his shop window.

Dragon
for sale –
only five
gold coins

Mopsy, Pete's helper, gave the dragon a bath. She got very wet. The dragon gave Mopsy's face a friendly lick. Then it burped. "Oh dear," said Pete, opening the window.

The shop bell rang to let them know they had a customer.

"I'm Chloe and I'd like to buy the dragon," the little girl said.

"How much money can you offer?" asked Pete.

"Two plastic pennies," said Chloe.

"You won't be able to buy *anything* with two plastic pennies," grumbled the Griffin.

Chloe looked upset. "I want a pet that will do magic tricks," she said.

"Actually," said Pete kindly, "I do have a very nice magic slug for two plastic pennies. Put it on a cabbage and it will make the cabbage disappear."

Chloe was very pleased with her slug.

Chapter 2
Dragon NOT For Sale

Pete put the plastic pennies into the cash box. He put his head into his hands. The day was not going well.

The dragon burped. The day was not getting any better.

Beware of fingers when feeding

Please wash hands, paws and claws.

BuRP

LOST DOG

Slugs for sale

Pete changed the sign.

The sign reads: Dragon for sale— only four gold coins

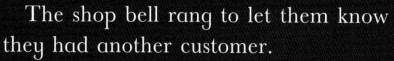

The shop bell rang to let them know
they had another customer.
   "I'm Lady Overtop. I'd be the envy of
all my friends if I had a dragon," she said.

Pete showed her the dragon. It peered
at her unhappily and burped loudly.

Lady Overtop promptly left the shop,
holding her nose.

Pete changed the sign.

Dragon
for sale –
only three
gold coins

A wizard entered. "Let me see the dragon," he demanded. He looked at it and said, "It's a bit on the small side for my needs. I will give you half a gold coin for it."

"What do you need it for?" asked Pete.

Beware
of fingers
when
feeding

"I need bits of dragon to carry out some spells," said the wizard.

"There will be no spells using *any* of my pets!" Pete shouted. He chased the wizard from the shop.

Pete's Peculiar Pet Shop

Pete's Peculiar Pet Shop

Dragon for sale – only three gold coins

"Oh dear," said Pete. "No one wants a sad-looking dragon that burps."

Pete took the sign out of the window.

Chapter 3
A Peculiar Cat

The dragon sat behind the counter on a fluffy blanket.

A bus stopped outside the shop and an old witch struggled down the steps.

"Can I help you, madam?" asked Pete.

"Please speak up, young lady," said the witch. "I'm very deaf." Her eyes did not work very well either.

"**My name is Pete**," shouted Pete. "**Can I help you?**"

"My hearing is not good.
My eyesight is worse," she said.
"I can't fly my broomstick, so
I don't go out much. I want a
nice fluffy cat to sit on my lap
and keep me company."

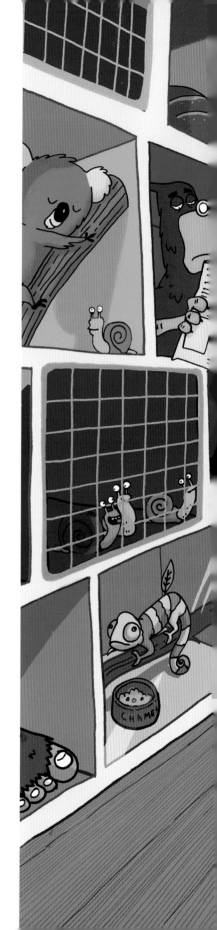

Pete looked around the shop. He had lots of peculiar pets. He even had friendly slugs, but he didn't have a fluffy cat.

Pete liked the witch and he wanted to help her. He carefully placed the dragon, with the fluffy blanket, onto the witch's lap.

"I only have this cat at the moment," he bellowed. "It's unusual and very smelly."

The dragon burped a very smelly burp.

"I have no sense of smell," said the witch, stroking the fluffy blanket.

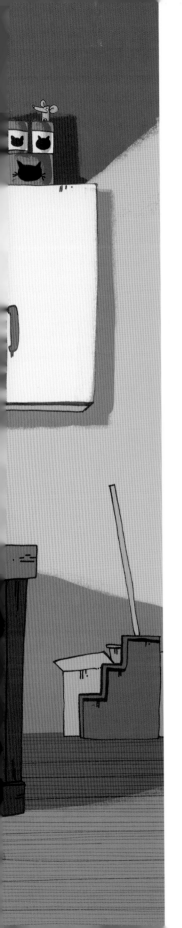

"This is a very unusual
cat. I'd be happy to look
after it." She winked at Pete.
"How much is it?"

"**It just so happens that this cat comes free if you buy one of our slugs**," yelled Pete.

"How much is a slug, then?" asked the witch.

"**Two plastic pennies**."

"Lovely," said the witch.

The witch took the dragon and the slug home. The dragon curled up on her lap with the blanket and she stroked it.

When the dragon got too big to fit on her lap, it crouched beside her chair. It rested its head on her lap so she could still stroke it.

The dragon was the best pet she could ever have asked for.

What's more, when the witch wanted to go out, she didn't need to catch the bus. Her peculiar cat could fly her anywhere.

Sometimes they took the slug along too, just for the ride.